Woodbourne Library
Washington-Centerville Public Library
Centerville, Ohio

W9-ACT-046

DISCARD

Clouds

A Level One Reader

By Alice K. Flanagan

Reader

The Child's World®

2

Look at the clouds. What colors and shapes do you see?

Clouds have three main shapes.

Some clouds are shaped like fluffy cotton balls.

These clouds sometimes bring rain and thunder.

10

Some clouds look like feathers or horses' tails.

Other clouds cover the sky like blankets or ocean waves.

Clouds form when tiny drops of water in the air join together.

The drops become too heavy to be held in the air. Then they fall as rain.

18

If the air is cold, the drops will fall as snow.

Can you tell what kind of weather the clouds will bring today?

Word List

blanket

cotton

feathers

fluffy

snow

thunder

weather

Note to Parents and Educators

Welcome to Wonder Books®! These books provide text at three different levels for beginning readers to practice and strengthen their reading skills. Additionally, the use of nonfiction text provides readers the valuable opportunity to *read to learn*, not just to learn to read.

These leveled readers allow children to choose books at their level of reading confidence and performance. Nonfiction Level One books offer beginning readers simple language, word choice, and sentence structure as well as a word list. Nonfiction Level Two books feature slightly more difficult vocabulary, longer sentences, and longer total text. In the back of each Nonfiction Level Two book are an index and a list of books and Web sites for finding out more information. Nonfiction Level Three books continue to extend word choice and length of text. In the back of each Nonfiction Level Three book are a glossary, an index, and a list of books and Web sites for further research.

State and national standards in reading and language arts emphasize using nonfiction at all levels of reading development. Wonder Books® fill the historical void in nonfiction material for the primary grade readers with the additional benefit of a leveled text.

About the Author

Alice K. Flanagan taught elementary school for ten years. Now she writes for children and teachers. She has been writing for more than twenty years. Some of her books include biographies, phonics books, holiday books, and information books about careers, animals, and weather. Alice K. Flanagan lives with her husband in Chicago, Illinois.

Published by The Child's World®
P.O. Box 326
Chanhassen, MN 55317-0326
800-599-READ
www.childsworld.com

Photo Credits
© Annie G. Belt/CORBIS: 13
© Christoph Wilhelm/CORBIS: 21
© Claire Hayden/Tony Stone: cover
© CORBIS: 17
© Eastcott Momatiuk/The Image Bank: 5
© Eye Wire/Getty Images: 6, 10
© G. Brad Lewis/Tony Stone: 18
© Julie Habel/CORBIS: 2
© National Geographic/Getty Images: 9
© Raymond Gehman/CORBIS: 14

Editorial Directions, Inc.: E. Russell Primm and Emily J. Dolbear, Editors;
Alice K. Flanagan, Photo Research; Emily J. Dolbear, Photo Selector

The Child's World®: Mary Berendes, Publishing Director

Copyright © 2003 by The Child's World®
All rights reserved. No part of this book may be
reproduced or utilized in any form or by any means
without written permission from the publisher.
Printed in the United States of America.

Library of Congress Cataloging-in-Publication Data
Flanagan, Alice K.
  Clouds / by Alice K. Flanagan.
    p. cm. — (Wonder books)
Summary: Describes the three main types of cloud formations
and how they appear.
Includes bibliographical references and index.
  ISBN 1-56766-450-4 (lib. bdg. : alk. paper)
1. Clouds—Juvenile literature. [1. Clouds.] I. Title.
II. Series: Wonder books (Chanhassen, Minn.)
  QC921.35 .F55 2003
  551.57'6—dc21
                          2002151513

24